Light the Lights!

ISBN 0-590-48383-8

Copyright © 1994 by Margaret Moorman.
All rights reserved. Published by Scholastic Inc.
SCHOLASTIC, CARTWHEEL BOOKS, and associated logos
are trademarks and/or registered trademarks of Scholastic Inc.

12 11 10 9 8 7 6 5 4 3   2 3 4/0

Printed in the U.S.A.   24
First Scholastic Trade paperback printing, October 1999

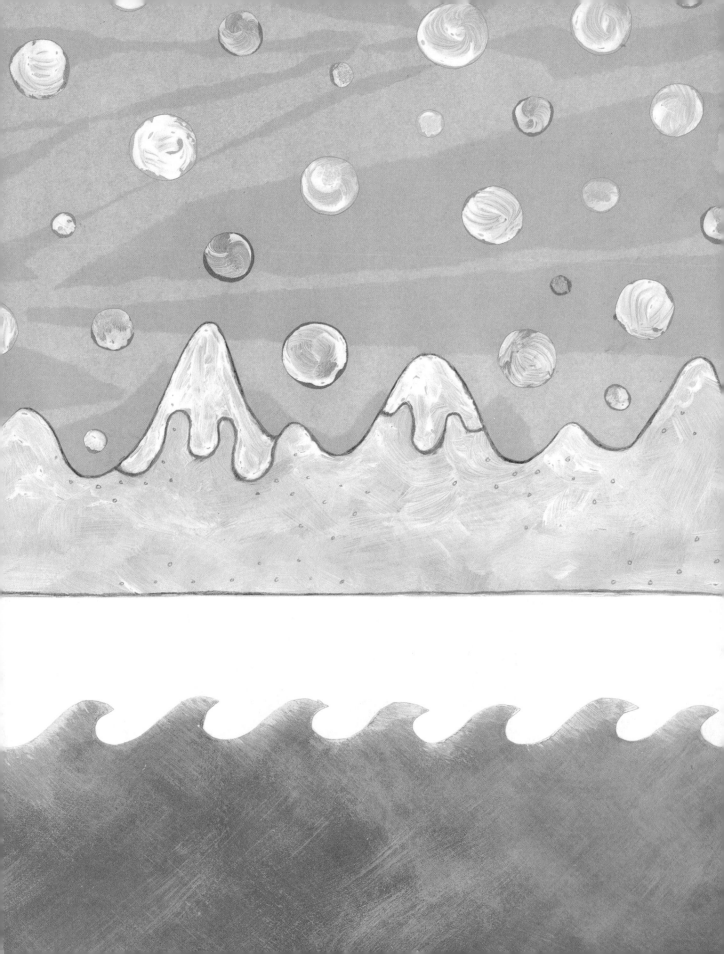

"Wow!" said Grandpa. "I wish I had tusks like yours."

"Dr. Tusker will make you a false tusk," said Wilbur. "You'll have to go to the dentist."

"I don't want to go to the dentist!" said Grandpa.

"Tsk-tsk," said Wilbur. He put his flipper around Grandpa's shoulder. "If I can go to the dentist, so can you!"

She gave Wilbur a sticker.
It said: "I brush my tusks."

"If you brush your tusks twice a day with this special fish-flavored toothpaste, your tusks will be strong and shiny," said Dr. Tusker.

"I see what the problem is," she said. "You've got a piece of a shell stuck in the top of your tusk. There! I've taken it out." "That feels much better!" said Wilbur.

Dr. Tusker, the dentist, was very gentle.

"Yes," said Wilbur. "I'll have
to go to the dentist!"
"Finally!" said
Mrs. Walrus.

Mrs. Walrus waddled up the landing slope toward them. "Walter and Wanda said I'd find you here," she said. "Is your tusk still hurting?"

Grandpa smiled. "Neither did I," he said.

"I don't want to go to the dentist,"
said Wilbur.

"Tsk-tsk," said Grandpa. He put his flipper around Wilbur's shoulders and helped him up onto the ice floe. "What is the matter?"

"My tusk hurts," Wilbur wailed.
His whiskers quivered.
"You'll have to go to the dentist," Grandpa said.

"I'll swim to Grandpa's," Wilbur said.
"It's easy to get out there. He's got
a landing slope."
It was a long way to Grandpa's.
Wilbur's tusk hurt in the cold water.
He pulled himself up Grandpa's landing
slope and lay there moaning.

Wanda poked her tusks into the ice
and pulled herself up onto the ice floe.
Wilbur poked his tusks into the ice and...

"Owww!" yelled Wilbur.

"My tusk hurts!"

"You'll have to go to the dentist,"
Wanda said.

"I don't want to go to
the dentist," said Wilbur.

Walter poked his tusks into the ice
and pulled himself up onto the ice floe.

Wanda, Wilbur, and Walter
swooped down the slide.

Splash!

They somersaulted into the sea.

"That was great!
Let's do it again!" Walter said.

"My tusk only hurts when I wrestle," said Wilbur.
"Let's play on the ice slide with Wanda."

Wheee!

Wilbur's friends were tusk wrestling.
Wilbur loved tusk wrestling.
He locked tusks with
his friend Walter.

Whump!

"Owww!" yelled Wilbur. "My tusk hurts!"
"You'll have to go to the dentist,"
Walter said.
"I don't want to go to the
dentist," said Wilbur.

"Have some seaweed," said Mrs. Walrus. "It's nice and soft."

"Ugh!" said Wilbur. "I don't want to eat seaweed. It's green and slimy."

"Then you'll have to go to the dentist," said Mrs. Walrus.

"I don't want to go to the dentist," said Wilbur.

"My tusk only hurts when I crunch,"
said Wilbur. "If I take off the shells,
I can just slurp them."

"I don't want to go to the dentist," said Wilbur.

Wilbur and his mother were crunching
their way through a huge pile of shellfish.
"Owww!" said Wilbur. "My tusk hurts!"
"You'll have to go to the dentist,"
Mrs. Walrus said.

Tooth Trouble

Written by Jane Clarke
Illustrated by Cecilia Johansson

SCHOLASTIC INC.

New York   Toronto   London   Auckland   Sydney
Mexico City   New Delhi   Hong Kong   Buenos Aires